The Magic Elf Christmas Massacre

MATTHEW VAUGHN

Other Books By Matthew Vaughn:

Paperbacks:

The ADHD Vampire

Mother Fucking Black Skull of Death - Revised Edition

The Survivors

Hellsworld Hotel

30 Minutes or Less – The Complete Story

Stories from the Hellsworld Hotel

The best deals on the E-books can be found at godless.com

The Sexual Avenger Series on Godless

Lucifer's Mansion (A Hellsworld Hotel Prequel)

Mephistophele's Den (A Hellsworld Hotel Prequel)

30 Minutes or Less

30 Minutes or Less Part 2

30 Minutes or Less Part 3

Rejects

Love Story

The Sexoricist

A Thanksgiving Story

The Magic Elf Christmas Massacre

Also :

The Classics Never Die! An Anthology of Old School Movie Monsters

Edited and Compiled by Edward and Matthew Vaughn

To Krystal, thanks for helping to keep our kids imagination alive.

Table of Contents

Chapter 1

Her tits were huge, not only were they massive, they were fucking going to give her horrible back trouble ginormous, which was why Stephen was fucking her. If it wasn't for her insanely big mommy milkers, maybe Stephen's good sense would kick in and he'd run, 'cause the girl was also fucking crazy as hell.

But she had the biggest tits he had ever seen in real life. They were not the biggest you've ever seen on a woman in the grocery store set of titties, they were seen on the Internet, random porn sites, comically big tits. So, needless to say, he was not thinking correctly, especially with these big-ass motherfuckers laying on either side of his head. She was on top of him, her ample ass bouncing up and down on his dick, and she was leaned over and her ginormous tetas laid like two extra heads on either side of his head.

As she rode on top of him she mumbled to herself and sometimes talked aloud some weird shit Stephen had never heard before. He thought for sure she had something wrong with her and as they fucked she was in the throws of an episode. The only word he did catch almost sounded like Baphomet, but twisted a little. Baephamete maybe? It was at that point he started becoming a little concerned about what was going on. But, then one of those big, ten inch around nipples would slide across his face and he'd forget all about the crazy shit she was spouting off.

Stephen had met her, Linda, online on a website called Freak Lifers. It was a website dedicated to people with various freaky kinks, and Stephen was on there constantly searching for women with the biggest hooters. He loved browsing various pictures of women who posted naked selfies with their big tits out. It was also a social media type site where you could friend and follow people on there. Stephen had friended Linda mainly because of her boobs. Over the course of a couple of months, they had become friendly enough with each other that they wanted to meet offline. Part of her kink was men in uniform, and it just so happened that Stephen was a security guard for a high-end toy store.

The other part of her kink was toys and not the adult kind one would normally pleasure themselves with. She liked to fuck surrounded by dolls and action figures, stuffed animals, and plastic toys. Stephen thought it was weird, he worried that this might have stemmed from some abuse she suffered as a child, but she had those super humongous titties so he looked past all that.

So there they were, banging it out in the middle of the Christmas toy aisle of the store, her titties flopping around, smacking him in the face. One hit him so hard it split his lip open and Linda laughed, so Stephen bit that titty. Not too hard, but enough that she knew he did it, and she fucking loved it. She grabbed his head and pulled his face in between those monsters, smothering him as she continued to bounce up and down on his dick.

"I'm fucking loving this!" She screamed at him. Stephen turned his head to one side, and with a mouthful of titty he said 'me too!'

"I feel it, I'm gonna cum any second now!" She shouted. Linda let Stephen's head fall to the floor, and fall it did. The back of his skull smacked hard against the tile.

"Ow fuck!" He let out, taking a hand from her meaty thigh and touching it to the back of his head. His hand came away wet and sticky. He was bleeding. "Holy shit, that fucking hurt."

Stephen looked up from his bloody hand into Linda's face, and then he saw the knife in her hand. His first thought was they were naked in a toy store, where the hell did she get that knife? Then she plunged it into his heart as she screamed out with her orgasm. Stephen screamed out at the same time, though his scream was considerably higher in pitch than hers.

At first, he lay there looking between the

knife handle sticking out of his chest and her huge tits as they jiggled while her body shuttered in ecstasy, He couldn't believe what just happened, he was frozen in fear and completely unsure of what to do in this situation. Linda seemed to calm down and look down at Stephen. She was smiling at him.

"I make this sacrifice to thee oh beloved Baephamete!" Linda yelled out, her voice booking in the empty store. "Please oh lord of Hell, continue to grant me favor as I send another human to be your eternal plaything!"

She moved quickly, so quickly that Stephen could not have stopped her even if he tried. Linda grabbed the hilt of the knife and ripped it from Stephen's chest. Blood immediately began to spray everywhere, it shot from the wound like a geyser. Stephen screamed out and blood filled his mouth. The fountain of blood caught Linda on her face and tits and she began rubbing it into the skin on her breast like it was the world's best lotion. She started grinding on top of Stephen even though at this point his cock had gone flaccid inside of her, but it didn't matter, his pubic bone right above his shaft was hitting in just the right place.

Linda continued massaging the blood into her tits and she rode Stephen's now dead body into a second orgasm. By that point, he had stopped spraying blood, but it was everywhere. His corpse was surrounded by a pretty big puddle, and a lot of the toys on both sides of the aisles had been doused pretty good as well. Linda stood up from Stephen's corpse, her knees popping loudly in the quiet store, and looked around for her clothes. They were nearby and pretty much covered in blood too. She didn't care, it wasn't like she was about to go and wash the blood off of her body or anything. She stepped into her black dress and if she gave a shit about it, you couldn't really see the blood all over it, but she had it all over her chest and face so it didn't matter.

When she pulled the dress up in place the blood-covered top of her massive titties was exposed for anyone to see. She knew she wouldn't be seeing anyone though.

One last look around the place to make sure she wasn't leaving anything incrementing behind and she was out the back service entrance door that Stephen had let her in earlier in the night. She had gotten everything she wanted from him, and that made this a successful night in her opinion.

On the shelf next to Stephen's cooling corpse, there was a box containing an elf doll dressed in a red outfit with a little red hat on his head. On the clear plastic covering the front of the box, splattered blood ran down in thin streaks.

In the quiet, empty toy store, the cardboard box shuttered.

Chapter 2

Tom walked into the toy store and immediately regretted it. He hated going to any stores on a good day but this was the Christmas season and that made everything that much worse. The store was cram fucking packed and hot as balls. This was one of Tom's least favorite things about the Christmas season, it was so cold outside that you had to dress warmly, then everywhere you went was hot as fuck and you were sweaty and uncomfortable the entire time. But, Tom was on a mission for one thing and one thing only, so he figured he could deal with all the bullshit, for a few minutes anyway.

This definitely wasn't his first trip to this

particular store, he knew the layout. He was on a mission and he walked into the store and headed directly where he knew he needed to go. Tom quickly walked around the old ass woman slowly moving through the aisles and dodged excited kids as they bounced around the place. Then he hit a roadblock.

As Tom confidently turned a corner and found that it was blocked off with caution tape strung from one set of shelves to the other, like this was some kind of crime scene no one was allowed to cross. He stopped and looked around, almost like he didn't believe what was happening. He could see down the aisle and right there on the left side, almost midway down, he saw what he wanted, The Magic Elf dolls.

"Can I help you?" a young voice said from behind Tom. He turned away from the aisle with the doll he needed to see a young, probably teen-aged, girl standing there. She wore a shirt emblazoned with the store logo, and a name tag that read - Hi, my name is Sam, how can I help you? - and had a Christmas hat on her head. She smiled brightly and Tom couldn't help but wonder how in the hell she could be that happy working in that god-forsaken store at Christmas time.

"Yeah, actually you can," he said to her, He pointed down the blocked-off aisle. "I need to get a Magic Elf doll for my son. What's up with this being blocked off?"

Sam scrunched her face up and looked like she wasn't exactly sure how to break some bad news to him.

"I'm sorry sir, we had an accident down there and now no one is allowed to go down there," she said to him. Tom noticed she had lowered her voice to say this.

He leaned in towards her slightly, almost conspiratorially.

"What do you mean an accident?" He asked. Sam quickly looked around. Tom thought she was probably a good kid who was more than likely instructed to lie to customers but was struggling with doing that. She leaned in a little towards him.

"Someone got hurt, one of our security

guards. This police sealed it off and that's why we can't have anyone go down there," Sam told him.

"You're shitting me," Tom said and glanced back down the aisle. "Well, that sucks."

"Yeah, it's kind of an inconvenience for sure," Sam said. "What was it you needed again?"

Tom turned back around to her.

"I need to get a Magic Elf doll for my son. He's been seeing the commercials lately and it's all he talks about," Tom said. Sam's face dropped a little.

"I'm so sorry sir, but those are the only ones we have, and we can't get to them right now. I'm pretty sure we'll have this back open in a couple of days if you can wait and just come back?"

Tom looked at the girl, she was very nice and he wasn't the kind of asshole that gets angry with the staff at a store when shit doesn't go his way. But there was no way in hell he was going to come back to this store in a couple of days if he could help it.

"Okay, cool. Well, thanks anyway," he

said to her with a smile. Sam beamed a big smile back to him.

"Yeah, no problem," she said as she started to move away from him, her attention being drawn to something else going on in the busy store. "If you need help with anything else, just ask!"

"Will do, thanks," Tom said and watched as she walked away and turned down the next aisle.

Tom didn't waste a second. He looked around, saw that no one was paying any attention to him, and turned and ducked under the tape that was strewn across the aisle to block it off. He walked quickly down the aisle, constantly turning and looking over his shoulder as he did. The Magic Elf's were about midway down, and they went from the bottom shelf to the top. Directly in front of the dolls was a curtain erected to block something, and before grabbing one of the dolls he had to satisfy his curiosity and look to see what it was covering up.

Conveniently, right where he was

standing, there was a split in the curtain, so all he had to do was lean forward and barely move one side of the curtain to look. Inside, there was more blood than he had ever seen before in his life covering the floor. He stepped back from the curtain, the huge puddle of red on the floor making his stomach feel a little queasy.

His mind had a ton of questions that he knew would probably never get answered. He quickly looked back down the aisle behind him, saw the coast was still clear, reached over and grabbed the closest doll off the shelf, and began walking back down toward the barrier at the end of the aisle.

Surprisingly, he made it out under the tape and no one saw him at all. He kept the doll close to his body just in case he ran into Sam and made a beeline for the cash registers. He stopped when they came into view, there was a huge ass line. He hung his head and walked to the back of it, seeing as he didn't have much of a choice.

The line actually moved faster than he had expected, which was a relief to Tom. He kept watching for Sam hoping she wouldn't walk by and bust him with the doll. Would she have said anything? What really could happen if she did? Could she what, get him thrown out of the store and then he would be forced to go to another one and do this all over again? Really, as weird as it was, he was more concerned about her seeing the doll, knowing what he did, and being disappointed with him. He didn't even know the girl, but she was nice so it made him feel weird.

Regardless, he made it to the checkout with no incident and sat the doll on the counter. That's when he saw it, blood on the front of the box. He was at a loss of what to do, surely the kid at the register would see it and know something was up. Tom looked from the clear plastic front dotted with red to the chunky boy at the register whose heavy eyes looked like he'd smoked a bit before coming into work today.

“Is this all?” the boy asked.

“Yeah, just this,” Tom said as he pulled his wallet out. The boy lifted a handheld price checker in one hand and tilted the elf doll forward with the other to zap the bar code on the bottom. The boy turned back to the register and punched some buttons on the screen. Tom stared at him with his card out, ready to swipe it through the reader.

"Alright man, that'll be forty-seven sixty-eight," the boy said as he looked up at Tom with a goofy grin.

Tom grimaced, he didn't even pay attention to how much this thing cost. 'Why the hell was it so expensive?' He thought. He stuck his card in the reader and let it do its thing while the boy produced a plastic bag from somewhere and slid it over the box. Once he had his card back in his wallet and the boy handed him his receipt, he grabbed the bag and breathed a sigh of relief. He was out the door and headed to his car, feeling pretty good about how well things worked out for him.

Once in his car, Tom pulled the box from the plastic bag and looked at the toy. What the hell had happened in that store for there to be all that blood pooled up on the floor, and there's blood on his elf's box? He didn't figure he would ever actually know, but regardless, he needed to clean the blood off of the box before he took it home.

Tom reached across the passenger seat and popped open his glove box, inside he found a stack of brown napkins from various fast food restaurants, those things always come in handy. He grabbed a few out and grabbed an old water bottle from the cup holder in his door. 'Score one for never cleaning your car out,' he thought to himself.

The combination of the water and the napkins worked really well to get the blood cleaned off, and when he was finished, he admired his handy work. He could see the elf doll in the box clearly now, its painted-on eyes looking perpetually to the left like it was spying something out of the corner of its eyes, and its smile that looked way more mischievous than just happy-go-lucky.

"Whatever," he said to the empty car and dropped the box into his passenger seat. It's what Jack, his son wanted, so he got it. Mission accomplished, he headed home.

Chapter 3

"Oh wow, so cool!" Jack said when his mom and dad gave him The Magic Elf doll. He held the box in his hands almost reverently, like it was a sacred object. He looked up at his parents with a smile that took up most of his face. "Thanks so much, I love it!"

"I'm glad honey," Jack's mom, Jill, says to him.

"Well, let's get it open and see what we need to do," Tom said, reaching for the box.

They had a vague idea of what to do, they had seen some YouTube videos after Jack kept mentioning wanting one. He pulled out his pocket knife and cut the tape that held the box flaps closed. Tom slid the doll attached to a cardboard backing out of the box and a little booklet came with it. Jill grabbed the booklet and opened it as Tom worked on getting the doll the rest of the way out of its secured packaging. Jack was on the edge of his seat watching his father work.

"It says here that you have to come up with a name for your elf, and then he will awaken tonight after we go to sleep and he'll fly back to Santa at the north pole," Jill said as she read the booklet aloud.

"Is he going to leave us?" Jack asked, a little confused as to how this whole thing worked.

"He'll come back before we wake up in the morning," Tom said as he finally removed the last tie holding the elf in place. He pulled the doll free. "There we go."

Jack's eyes lit up as he reached out for the elf. Tom handed it over to him.

"This is the only time you get to touch him," Jill said. "Once you name him and he gets his magic, you can't touch him or he loses his magic."

Jack nodded his head but he was looking at the doll and was barely paying attention to her at all.

"I want to name him Butter-snap," Jack said. Tom winced and looked over at Jill and mouthed Butter-snap with a disgusted look on his face. She shook her head and mouthed he's five, shut the fuck up. Tom laughed and looked back to Jack.

"Okay then, Butter-snap it is. Let's set him up on the fireplace mantle while we sleep and let him get his magic and go see Santa. Jack reluctantly agreed to give the doll up and the three of the walked over to the fireplace and set the doll up so that it looked like he was sitting there waiting on something.

"Alright Jack, let's go get those teeth brushed so you can get in bed," Jill said, and they watched as Jack ran off down the hall.

"He is really happy to get this thing," Tom said to her. She turned and looked at him.

"You did good picking it up today, I was worried they were going to be sold out or something," Jill said.

"Yeah, the store was busy as fuck too, it pretty much sucked," Tom said to her with a smile. She smiled back and pushed her body against his.

"Maybe I can do something to reward you for your bravery today," she said to him.

"Oh yeah?" Tom said and leaned down and kissed her.

After Jack brushed his teeth and they tucked him into bed, Tom grabbed a couple of beers from the fridge and they took them to their bedroom. They turned their TV on under the premise that they might watch a little something, but they didn't pay attention to it at all, it was just background noise to them while they made love.

After a while, Jill got up to use the bathroom so Tom grabbed their empty beer bottles and left the bedroom to go to the kitchen and get them some new drinks.

Tom walked down the stairs to the first floor, and before he made his way to the kitchen he happened to glance across the living room, over at the fireplace mantle. He stopped and looked for a minute. Butter-snap the elf was now sitting on the other side of the mantle from where he had placed him earlier in the night.

"Huh, that's weird," he said aloud. Tom walked over to the mantle and looked at the little toy elf. He was positioned differently than he had been, His legs were crossed over one another like he was kicked back relaxing. Its head was turned so that the eyes that looked to one side were actually looking at him.

'Jill must have preemptively moved him thinking we might forget to do it before we fell asleep.' he thought to himself.

"She could have come up with something a little more creative," he said aloud to no one. He turned from the elf and made his way to the kitchen, where he threw the empty bottles away and grabbed two fresh beers before heading back upstairs to their bedroom. The two of them ended up drinking four beers a piece and watching a horror movie before they finally went to sleep for the night.

At about three in the morning, Tom woke to a sound. He was pulled from a deep sleep that left him momentarily confused. He looked over to his left and was startled by Jack standing there.

"Holy crap Jack, you scared me. What's up buddy?" Tom asked him, his heart racing now.

"Something is in my room," the boy said to him. Tom looked at him for a moment.

"What do you mean something is in your room?" Tom asked. He threw the covers off himself knowing that no matter what, he would have to walk his son back to his room before he would be able to go back to sleep.

"I don't know, I heard something moving around, it woke me up," Jack said, and Tom noticed he was on the verge of tears. He pulled his son to him.

"Hey, hey, it's okay buddy. We can walk down there and check it out," Tom said, comforting him.

"Do you think it's Butter-snap?" Jack asked. Tom pulled away and looked at him.

"Wouldn't that be a good thing if it was?

That just means he's come back from the north pole, from talking to Santa."

"No, I don't know. I'm scared," the boy said. Tom knew Jack was kind of afraid of just about everything, but he hadn't thought of the possibility of him being afraid of The Magic Elf that he wanted so badly.

"Come on buddy, let's go see what we can find," Tom said, standing up from the bed. He took Jack by the hand and walked him out of the bedroom, down the hallway, and to his bedroom.

Once inside Jack's bedroom, Tom turned on the light so they could look around. He did the obligatory checking of the closet, under the bed, and any of the normal places he would typically look for the boogeyman. Jack watched all of this from where he sat on the bed, cross-legged.

"I don't see anything buddy, I think maybe you had a bad dream or something," Tom said as he lifted himself from the floor and walked over to where Jack sat. "Everything is fine in here, you don't have anything to worry about. Lay down, and go back to sleep."

The boy nodded and crawled back under his covers. Tom tucked him in, kissed him on his head, and left the room. He walked back into his bedroom and tried to gently slip back into bed, under the covers. Jill stirred next to him.

"Everything okay?" she said to him, just barely out of sleep.

"Yeah, he got scared, thought the elf might be in his room," Tom said. He looked over to Jill, but she was already fast asleep. He smiled at her, then turned over and waited for sleep to take him too.

Laying in his bed with the covers pulled up to his chin, Jack closed his eyes and tried to go back to sleep, but he was still terrified. His dad coming into his room and checking to make sure nothing was in there did little to ease his child's mind. He knew what had happened, he knew the elf had been in there with him.

As he lay there in the dark he heard another noise, followed by the creaking of his door moving. He looked quickly at the door and saw it slowly moving and shut his eyes again, tight. Moments later he felt his covers move slightly like something was pulling on them as it climbed up the side of his bed. Then he felt the little feet walking up his body.

"Hey you little mother fucker, you little snitch bitch," a voice said to him. It was so much more aggressive and angry compared to what Jack would have thought an elf's voice would sound. "Open your eyes you little cock sucker."

Jack did as he was told and opened his eyes. The elf was right there, on his little chest and staring directly into his face.

"You ratted me out you little snitch bitch. I outta fucking gut you right here and now," the elf said to him. Jack started to cry. He tried to shrink away from the elf, but there was nowhere for him to go. "Oh God, now I have to watch you cry like a little girl? Jezuz fuck me, I can't believe this shit. For some reason, it seems I'm bonded to you, so I can't fucking kill you and drape myself in your entrails like I want to. So fucking relax you little piece of shit. Believe me, I want to so bad, naming me Butter-snap, what the fuck kinda lame ass name is that? But I sure as fuck can do something to your lame-ass parents. Speaking of which, I might not have a dick right now, but I'd sure like to show your mom how a real man fucks. I know your pussy ass dad ain't giving it to her right. I'll rape her ass and make her my bitch, mark my words."

Jack was so scared by that point he was shaking.

"Go the fuck to sleep you little piece of shit. And don't tell your fucking dad about me again, that takes all the fun out of what's coming."

With that, Butter-snap turned and walked down the length of Jack's body and jumped off the side of his bed. Jack pulled his covers up over his head and laid there, shaking, until some time in the night when he finally fell asleep.

Chapter 4

"Tom," Jill said to Tom's back. Tom was combing his hair in the mirror and looked over his shoulder at his wife. “Jack is acting really weird about the elf today. It's like he's scared of it or something.”

Tom finished styling his short hair and sat the cob down on the sink and turned to his wife.

“Do you remember him waking us up last night talking about it being in his room?” he asked her as he walked from the bathroom into their bedroom to grab a tie from the closet.

“Vaguely, I was pretty out of it last night,” Jill said. She sat on the edge of the bed and watched her husband getting ready.

“Yeah, I was explaining it to you and you fell back asleep on me. He said he thought the elf was in his room last night, he was all freaked out about it,” Tom said, fixing his tie around his neck while he talked. “I think he just had a nightmare, maybe his excitement about the elf was screwing with his subconscious or whatever.”

"Maybe he’s still just shaken up by the whole thing,” Jill said, standing and walking over to Tom to help him straighten his tie. “I just hate how he's acting. He was so excited about that damn thing, now he won't even look at it much less talk about it.”

“Well, hopefully, he'll get over it today and eventually forget about his nightmare or whatever,” Tom said. Satisfied that he was finally ready, the pair exited their bedroom and went downstairs to where Jack sat watching TV in the kitchen. Tom pulled out a chair across from him and sat down, Jack didn’t even glance away from the cartoon on the TV.

“Hey bud, you okay?” Tom asked him. Jack nodded and kept on watching his cartoons.

"You sure? You seemed pretty scared last night."

"I'm okay," Jack said, emotionless. Tom looked up at Jill and shrugged.

"Your mom and I are getting ready to run out for a little while," Tom said, standing up from the table.

"Shelby is coming over to sit with you while we're gone," Jill said as she went to the refrigerator. She opened one door and pulled a bottle of water out when the doorbell rang. "I bet that's her now."

"I'll go get it," Tom said. He looked down at Jack who just continued to stare at the TV. "You stay there, don't bother getting up." He said with a grin.

Tom walked through the living room as he made his way to the door and he couldn't help glancing at the mantle where the elf was sitting. It was still in the same spot, on the edge of the mantle with its legs dangling over the side. Tom stopped for a second and looked at it, 'was it in the same spot from last night?' he thought to himself, The doorbell went again.

"I thought you were getting that?" Jill called out. Tom pulled himself away from the elf, shaking his head.

"I am, honey," he said as he continued to walk to the door.

Pulling the door open Tom saw Shelby standing there. She was young, early twenties, with hair dyed solid black. She dressed in solid black and was what Tom and Jill assumed was a goth, but she had grown up living next to them for years and they considered her family.

"Hey," she said to Tom as he stood to the side to let her in.

"Good morning, Shelby," Tom said. He shut the door and turned to follow her into the house. Tom couldn't help checking out her ass as they walked. She was nowhere near fat, but her ass had gotten big as she grew up, and Tom was very much an ass man. Tom was never inappropriate around her, and he would never try to do anything to the girl, but she had grown up to be pretty hot in Tom's eyes. 'If only I were a good fifteen years younger,' he thought.

"Hey Shelby, thanks for sitting for us so we can go out today. We shouldn't be more than a couple of hours," Jill said when Shelby and Tom walked into the kitchen. Shelby ruffled Jack's hair as she walked past him and pulled out a chair to sit down next to him.

"Yeah, we have to get back and get ready for the big Christmas party tonight," Tom said. He grabbed his jacket off the coat hook and slid it on. "So we need you to make sure Jack gets a bath while we are out please."

Tom pulled Jill's coat off the hook and had it opened up for his wife to step into.

"Are you listening Jack?" Jill said, sliding her arms into her coat while Tom held it open. "We need you to get your bath while we're gone. Listen to Shelby when she tells you it's time."

Once she had the coat on Tom reached into his front pocket and pulled out two twenty-dollar bills.

"Get you two some pizza later if you get hungry. With traffic and how crowded everything is, I'm sure we won't be back until after lunch," he said setting the money down on the counter. Shelby nodded as she watched the cartoons on the TV too. Jill kissed Jack on the top of the head and Tom patted his arm.

"We love you, Jack, we'll be back soon," Jill said to him. He finally pulled himself away from the TV to acknowledge their leaving.

"Love you guys too, see you in a little while," he said as he watched them walk to the front door. Tom pulled the door open to let Jill walk out, turned and waved at Jack and Shelby, then followed his wife out of the house.

Shelby turned from the front door and looked at Jack, who was back to staring at the cartoons on the TV. She nudged him with her elbow.

"What's up with you today, little man? You seem kind of mopey," she said to him. He didn't look at her.

"Nothing," he said. She didn't think it was nothing, he was usually excited and hyper when she came over. Today he seemed different. She looked around thinking about what they could do, wondering if they played a game or something would it cheer him up. Then, she noticed the elf on the mantle. Shelby pushed her chair back from the table and stood up. She walked into the living room and stopped in front of The Magic Elf.

"Is this one of those Magic Elf's?" she asked over her shoulder.

"Yes, don't touch it!" Jack yelled. She heard the feet of his chair scoot across the floor.

"I know, they lose their magic if you touch them, right?" she asked, and then he was right there next to her.

"No, I mean yes, but," he started then stopped. Shelby looked down at him, he seemed unsure about what he was trying to say. "He's really real. And he's bad."

Shelby looked back up at the doll, in his little red outfit with his little Santa hat on its head, he looked like just a doll to her.

"What do you mean he's bad? They're supposed to be mischievous or whatever," She said.

"No, he's really bad. He said really bad

things to me last night, I think he wants to hurt mom and dad," Jack said. He reached up and took hold of Shelby's hand. She looked back down at him, 'What the hell was he talking about?' This seemed like more than just some wild imagination, Jack didn't usually talk like this, he was an all-bubbly and fun-going kid.

"What do you mean wants to hurt your mom and dad?" she asked. He looked up at her, then past her. His little eyes went wide. Shelby turned from him and back to the doll. The elf was standing on the mantle, looking directly at her.

"What the fuck?" she said, taking a step back.

"You just had to fucking say something, didn't you? You little snitch bitch fucker," the elf said, his eyes boring into Shelby with an intensity of anger. "Boy I wish I could kill your pussy ass, you just can't keep that bitch ass mouth shut, can you? But dammit if this isn't some fine-looking pussy right here. I think I can let your bullshit go, for now, 'cause this juicy bitch is going to get all of my attention for now."

Shelby looked down at Jack almost as if she didn't believe what she was seeing and needed the validation of another person for her to understand this was real. Jack's reaction was plenty of validation, he looked scared shitless. It helped that he was seeing this too because her mind couldn't grasp onto what was happening, she couldn't get her shit together enough to realize she needed to run. She needed to grab Jack and get the hell out of there. Instead, she turned back to the elf, still expecting it to have been some kind of hallucination or the after-effects of tripping with her friends the past weekend. But he was still standing there looking at her, his little face scrunched up in anger, showing emotions that no doll with a painted on face should be able to show.

Shelby watched in shocked amazement as the thing turned to its right and picked up a snow globe of a little house that was decorated for Christmas, with lights and an inflatable Santa in the front yard. She focused on that snow globe for whatever reason, watching the tiny white flakes they put in them float around in the clear liquid as the elf lifted the snow globe over its head. Absurdly she marveled at the strength of such a little doll, 'How could it possibly be doing that?' she wondered to herself. Then, the little man in red leaped from the mantle and hit her in the head with the snow globe and she went lights out, her legs crumbling underneath her as she fell unconscious to the floor.

Chapter 5

Shelby's eyes slowly fluttered open. Her vision was blurred at first, but as she blinked things began to come into focus. Her natural reaction was to rub the sleep from her eyes, but she couldn't move her arms, they were pulled above her head and when she tried to move them they wouldn't budge like they were restrained.

"What the fuck?" she said aloud as she turned her head to look up at her hands. They were definitely restrained, tied to what looked like the headboard of a bed. That's when Shelby started looking around her, the panic beginning to sink in. She was in a bed, and she was naked, and her legs were just as restrained as her arms were.

"No, seriously, what the fuck is going on?"

She began to pull and struggle with her bindings as she flopped around on the bed. She wasn't getting any closer to being free though. She stopped and tried to calm her breathing, she needed to figure out what was going on here. She needed to not freak the fuck out and try to find a way out of this, whatever this was, but she was not doing a good job. She felt the freaking the fuck out building up inside her. So she closed her eyes again and just breathed. It helped her, she was calming some. Shelby realized her forehead was throbbing. She opened her eyes again and started looking around. She saw the Avengers and Minecraft posters on the walls and knew immediately she was in Jack's room.

She lifted her head and looked down the length of her naked body, in between her legs that were pulled apart and tied to the ends of the footrest, and saw Jack sitting against the wall. He had his hands covering his face and his little body hitched like he was crying.

"Jack, Jack," Shelby said. He didn't look

up. “What the hell is going on?”

“Goody, you're awake now,” a voice said. She recognized it but couldn’t place who it was. She looked around as she felt something pulling the skin on her thigh. She looked down and saw the elf climb up onto her leg. “I guess I hit you harder than I meant to. I thought you were going to wake up while I was yanking your clothes off of you. But you didn’t, and you didn’t while I was tying you to the pussy boy's bed.”

As the elf talked he walked up Shelby's naked body, and goosebumps crept across her flesh. He stopped in between her breasts, two small mounds on her chest that ended in short, erect, nipples. He was closer to the left breast.

“You don’t have much in the titty department, I like my women to have some big fucking tits. But, seeing as I don’t have any bitches with big tits hanging out around here right now, your itty bitty titties will have to do,” the elf said. He reached over and grabbed the nipple on Shelby’s left breast, wrapped his tiny hand around it and stroked it like a hard cock. “And let's be honest, I've never seen bad titties, I like them all. Hell, I even like saggy tits hanging down to your knees. I'll still play with them fuckers."

Shelby watched wide-eyed as the elf quit stroking her nipple and then opened his tiny mouth and took the nipple into its mouth. He was sucking on it like it was a hard dick too, his little hands massaging the dark areola. She winced as he bit down, not enough to bite the nipple off, but hard enough that when he lifted his head off he had blood in his mouth. He smiled up at Shelby and she was horrified about what he was getting ready to do to her.

"Open your eyes, kid," the elf said as he turned away from Shelby. He walked down her naked body and stopped at the top of her shaven mound. "I'm getting ready to teach you some things you ain't gonna learn from school. Though, looking at your dad, he's probably already teaching you some of this at night while your moms asleep!" The elf let out a gut-busting laugh at himself.

Jumping down from Shelby's pubic

mound, Butter-snap landed in between her spread legs. He turned and looked up at the smooth skin of her lips, leaned forward, and licked across the soft, smooth flesh. Shelby fought at her restraints again but it didn't do any good.

"I'm serious you little bitch, you better open your eyes and watch this, or your moms getting it next," the elf said, not turning to look at Jack to make sure that he was doing what he was told. He knew he didn't need to, he knew the threat against his mom would be enough to scare him into watching.

Butter-snap was right, and Jack slowly lifted his head just enough so his tear-filled eyes were looking over his arms wrapped around his knees. As he watched, the elf pulled apart Shelly's lips, exposing her insides to himself and the boy.

"Oh this going to be like throwing a hot dog down a hallway you fucking slut," the elf said. "If I had my normal body, I'd have a huge ass dick that would still split you in two. I don't, so I have to make do."

Without another word, the elf rammed his

head into Shelby's pussy, pointy hat first. She cried out in shock and pain as the head of the elf penetrated her while Jack screamed out in shock and surprise. The elf pushed himself into the girl, forcing himself through as his cloth hat and plastic face scraped against her dry vaginal walls. His shoulders entered her as he pushed further in, Shelby buckled and squirmed, but Butter-snap continued forcing himself into her. At about halfway in he pulled himself back out.

"You like that huh? I know you do you little whore," he said before ramming himself back into her. He pushed in deeper, to his waist before pulling himself back out and penetrating her again. He did this over and over, pushing himself in to his feet as he raped her with his little body, tearing her insides with each thrust.

When he felt satisfied, he pulled himself out from her cunt and stood in between her spread legs. He was slick and wet, covered in her pussy juice and blood. He turned to Jack, who sat horrified by the ordeal.

"Now that is how you pleasure a woman,"

Butter-snap said as he looked at the boy. Jack turned away, the slimy, grinning elf pulling himself from inside Shelby was the stuff of nightmares to the little boy.

Turning away from Jack, the elf picked up something thin and metallic that was laying on the bed, climbed back up Shelby's leg, and walked up her body toward her head. What he had was a fingernail file with a sharp, curved tip for cleaning out underneath the nails that he drug behind him as he walked. He left little feet prints of blood and a faint pink line from the file along her thigh and her stomach as he went. He stopped at her midsection, just above her belly button.

"Sup baby, you liked that?" Shelby didn't lift her head to look at him, she just stared blankly at the ceiling. "Yeah, I know you did, you don't have to say anything, I can tell."

Without warning, the elf pushed the file into Shelby's flesh, a bubble of blood appearing around the tip as he punctured the skin. She became alive then as she screamed out from the pain. Butter-snap drug the file down, pulling it toward her groin as it ripped through her flesh.

"I want to make sure everybody knows you're mine now," he grunted as he pulled the file to his right, arching it around. Her stomach was a pool of blood, and as she thrashed from the pain, the blood spilled down her sides. "Calm down, you're going to mess this up. If it ends up looking like shit it'll be your fault."

Tears poured from Shelby's eyes as Butter-Snap continued digging the metal blade into her flesh, carving across her from one side to the other. Every time he finished a line, the elf would stab the file into her again to start a new line. Shelby cried out each time, and Jack flinched from the sound, his hands pressed tightly against his ears. He was crying too, but his quiet sobs were nothing compared to Shelby's wailing in pain, her voice cracking as she begged and pleaded for the small elf to stop what he was doing to her.

Once he was finished he admired his work. A giant, bloody B S was carved into her stomach from the bottom of her rib cage to her abs. Shelby had quit fighting and laid still on the bed, her breathing harsh and ragged.

Chapter 6

"That took way longer than I expected," Tom said as he entered the front door of the house. He held the door open allowing Jill to come through after him.

"Well, it's just that time of the year. You know how it is out there, you can't expect things to move fast," Jill said to him.

"I know, I know. It's just that we only have a couple of hours to get ready for the party tonight," Tom said.

They walked into the living room and looked around. Tom couldn't help but glance to the mantle, to the elf sitting there exactly as it did when they were leaving. He felt like he was being watched by that thing.

“Jack,” Jill said. “We're home baby.”

Tom absentmindedly helped Jill take off her coat and watched as she headed for the staircase heading up to Jack’s room. Tom laid her coat on the couch and shrugged his own off, glancing toward the elf again as he did so. He noticed something odd about the elf, he had something on him. Tom tossed his coat on the couch as he walked toward the elf to get a better look. Just as he stepped toward the mantle he heard his wife's concerned voice.

“Jack, what are you doing what's wrong? Shelby is everything OK?”

Tom listened, his head turned away from the elf. ‘What's going on?’ he wondered to himself.

“Shelby, Shelby,” Jill said. He then heard the sound of someone walking down the steps. Tom turned away from the mantle and started moving to the staircase when Shelby came quickly down.

“Hey what's going on?” Tom asked her.

Shelby didn't acknowledge him and walked right past him toward the front door. “Hey, don't you want your money I've got your cash right here.”

Shelby didn't acknowledge him, she kept her head down and her arms wrapped around herself as she walked to the door, opened it, and was gone in a matter of seconds.

Tom watched her leave. Confused, he turned away and started heading upstairs to Jack's room.

“What's going on honey?” Tom said aloud as he turned the corner and entered Jack's room. Jack was sitting on the floor cross-legged and staring out into space. Jill was kneeling in front of him and she turned from the boy to look up at Tom.

“I don't know why he's like this,” Jill said. "And Shelby was pretty much doing the same thing but when I walked into the room she jumped up and ran out.” Jill turned and pointed behind her to the other side of the room.

“And there's no covers on his bed, his sheets are gone. I don't know what's going on, he won't talk to me," Jill said.

Tom looked at the bed Jill was pointing at, then back to the boy. He was confused by the situation, nothing was making any sense.

"Jack," Tom said low and slow. "Jack buddy, did something happen in here? Did something happen with Shelby while we were gone?"

"Did something happen with Shelby?" Jill said as she stood up and turned away from Jack to look at Tom. "What does that mean? What do you think happened?"

"I'm not saying anything did, it's just, with the sheets missing, I don't know? Its just the first place my mind went," Tom said, struggling to figure it all out.

Jill grabbed Tom's arm and pulled him out of the room.

"You think she did something to him, is that what you're saying?" She asked him once they were out in the hallway.

"Fuck I don't know Jill, what am I supposed to think? He won't talk to us and tell us anything."

Jill turned from Tom and looked toward Jack's bedroom.

"How about I'll get him in the bathtub, maybe I can see something or I can get him to talk to me."

Tom nodded his head.

"Okay, yeah, that sounds like a good idea," he looked around like he was trying to find something. "I'm just going to go downstairs and get a drink."

Tom looked at his watch.

"The Ferris' will be here before we know it. They're always showing up super early."

"Do you think we should cancel?" Jill asked, halfway into Jack's room.

"No, hell, I don't know," Tom thought for a moment before he spook again. "Let's just play it by ear for now and if we figure something out, we will take care of it."

Jill nodded to her husband and then disappeared into Jack's room. Tom left out of the hallway and made his way downstairs. He walked into the living room and picked up their coats on the couch and hung them up. After, in the kitchen, he poured himself a screwdriver and did his best to tidy up the place.

Periodically he went upstairs to check on Jill and Jack. She had bathed the boy and got him in clean clothes. There was no change in his mildly catatonic state. They put new sheets on his bed and laid him down, tucking him in. Tom held Jill while they stood there looking down at the boy. After a while, the doorbell rang and Tom disappeared downstairs to answer it.

"Hey there Tommy!" Evan Ferris said when Tom pulled the door open.

"Hello Evan, Trisha," Tom said to the couple on the porch. He stepped aside and gestured for the pair to come in. "Come on in guys, get out of the cold."

Evan and Trisha Ferris were a little older than Tom and Jill, with all their children grown and moved away. Evan and Tom worked together and had been working together for a few years. They walked into the house and Tom helped

Trisha out of her coat while Evan shrugged his own off.

"The temperature really dropped today," Evan said. Tom gathered their coats from them.

"Yeah, we were out in it earlier and it wasn't too bad, then bam, it was freezing," Tom said as he walked to the coat closet to put the coats away. "That's the good thing about throwing parties at your own house!"

"Yeah, I can differently see that!" Evan said.

"Where's Jill?" Trisha asked as she walked around the living room looking at recent pictures on the walls.

"She's upstairs with Jack. He, uh, hasn't been feeling well," Tom said, as he stepped back into the living room. "Do you all want a drink?"

"I thought you'd never ask," Evan said, turning to Tom. Jill turned from the newest Christmas picture of Jack.

"Yes, that sounds great," she said. "This picture of Jack is great, he's just so cute."

"Yeah, thanks. It's a good thing he looks

like his mother," Tom said with a laugh. Evan and Trisha laughed too and followed Tom into the kitchen.

"What are you drinking?" Evan asked. "A screwdriver?"

"Yeah, I picked up this vodka from a local distillery, it's pretty good," Tom said. He walked over to the counter and picked the bottle up, displaying it to Evan. He squinted and leaned forward where he was at.

"I'll take one of those then," Evan said, pulling a bar stool out from the island in the middle of the kitchen. Tom sat the vodka bottle down and pulled a glass from the cupboard over his head. He poured in two shots of Vodka before going to the fridge and getting the orange juice out. Once he fixed Evan's drink, he turned and slid it to the man across the island. Tom turned and looked at Trisha.

"Do you have any wine?" Trisha asked. She stood next to Evan at the Island.

"Yeah, let me run downstairs and grab some," Tom said as he walked to the basement door.

“Sit down,” Evan said to Trisha as he pulled out the stool next to him.

“I'm okay, I feel like standing right now,” she said. Evan shrugged and sipped some of his screwdriver.

“Oh yes, this is nice,” he said and took another sip. “Here, you should try it.”

“No thank you, orange juice gives me heartburn,” she said, shaking her head. Evan shrugged again.

“Your loss,” he said. He took another drink. “This is damn good.”

“Slow down, you’ll be drunk and pissing yourself before the night is over.”

Tom appeared at the basement door with two bottles of wine, one red and one white. He opened his mouth to say something when the doorbell rang again.

“Here, I’ll take care of the wine so you can get the door,” Trisha said, walking around the island to where Tom was.

“Thanks,” he said and sat the wine bottles

down on the counter.

"Where is your corkscrew?" Trisha called out as Tom disappeared from the kitchen. She looked up to see he had gone and shrugged. She began pulling open drawers in the counter and looking through them.

As Tom passed by the staircase, he saw Jill coming down. He stopped and looked up at her as she made her way down the stairs.

"How is he doing?" he asked her.

"He's still not talking. He's asleep now, hopefully, if he gets some sleep maybe he'll feel like talking," Jill said as she reached the bottom. The doorbell sounded again and they both looked toward the front of the house.

"I'll get the door," Tom said. "Evan and Trisha are in the kitchen if you want to go say hi."

Jill nodded and turned toward the kitchen as Tom started toward the front door again. Tom opened the door to see Seth and Carol York standing on their porch.

"Tom! Hey O!" Seth said with enthusiasm.

"Hey Seth, Carol, come on in," Tom said,

He held the door for them as they walked into his home.

"Oh boy, does it feel toasty in here," Seth said, slapping his mittened hands together. "I don't know when you were out last, but it is freezing outside."

"I was just telling Evan that we were out earlier today and it wasn't too bad, but the temperature started dropping quickly," Tom said as he began helping Carol with her coat.

"Evan and Trisha are here already?" Seth said as he shrugged his coat off. "I told you, Carol, that I thought I saw their car out there didn't I?"

"Yes, yes, dear. You know they always get here earlier than everyone else," Carol said as she straightened her sweater.

"Well, they're in the kitchen with Jill if you want to join them. I'll hang your coats up," Tom said.

"Come on honey, let's get in there before Evan drinks everything and there's nothing left for the rest of us," Seth said with a laugh.

“Oh Seth, you're too much sometimes,” Carol said. Seth put his arm around his wife and turned to guide her into the kitchen when he stopped.

“Hey, what's with the elf? You all decorating with Jack’s toys now?” Seth said with a laugh. He seemed to think everything he said was funny. Tom stopped walking with their coats in his arms and turned to the couple.

“Oh, that is a Magic Elf. He's a scout elf that Santa sends down from the north pole and he reports back how Jack acts up until Christmas.”

“Isn't that something,” Carol said.

“Does he only stay in here?” Seth asked.

“Well, he flies back to the north pole every night, so when he comes back he’s supposed to hide in a different place for Jack to find him in the morning when he gets up,” Tom said. He turned away from them and made his way to the coat closet.

“I hope he doesn’t decide to hide in the bedroom if you know what I mean!” Seth cried out, laughing at himself again. “He might report back to Santa how naughty you two are!"

"Oh Seth, you're just nasty," Carol said, smacking his arm playfully. They walked into the Kitchen with Tom following behind them, shaking his head.

While everyone was making their greetings and more drinks were being poured, the doorbell rang again and Tom went to answer it, again. He glanced at the elf as he walked by and couldn't help thinking there was something he was forgetting. He ignored the feeling and answered the door, letting Randal and Kelly Kirkwood in. Tom ushered them in, took their coats, and walked them into the kitchen to join the others.

Chapter 7

While the adults were in the kitchen enjoying their drinks and their conversations, Jack lay in his bed, in the dark with the covers pulled up to his chin. He had his eyes closed but he was awake. He heard his bedroom door open and assumed it was his mother. He was glad, he wanted to tell her what had happened, tell her all about how evil Butter-snap was. He was afraid to tell her, afraid of what the evil little elf would do, but he knew he had to tell her. He opened his eyes to look at her but he didn't see anyone. Then he felt that familiar tugging on his blankets and tensed up in anticipation of who he knew it would be. He closed his eyes tight, hoping the elf would go away and leave him alone.

“There's quite the party happening downstairs, shit face,” he heard Butter-snap say. He could feel the little elf walking up his body toward his head. “I know you ain't sleeping you little piece of shit. I gotta say, I'm impressed you didn’t rat on me to your parents, about me fucking that hot piece of ass you had over earlier today.”

Jack slowly opened his eyes and saw the elf an inch away from his face. He jumped and let out a surprised gasp. Butter-snap started laughing.

“I think I'm going to have some fun tonight,” the elf said, pacing around on Jack’s chest. “I'm going to fuck up your parent's friends, and then, I might just burn this whole fucking place down. What do you think about that?”

Jack stared at the elf silently for a moment.

”Why?” Jack finally said. The elf stopped moving and turned to look at the boy. “Why are you doing these things? You’re supposed to be a scout elf for Santa, why are you so mean?”

"I ain't no scout elf for Santa, I only serve

one master and that's Beaphamete," Butter-snap said. He got closer to Jack, who tried to shrink away but was trapped by his bed. "I'm a fucking spawn of Satan, I'm an ass-raping, mean motherfucker from hell. I don't know why I'm here, I don't know why I'm bonded to you, but I'm taking full advantage of the situation. And by that, I mean I'm having me some motherfucking fun."

The elf turned then and walked back down Jack's torso.

"You're probably going to want to stay up here, hiding under your covers and pissing your pants, 'cause shit is about to get bloody." With that, he jumped off the side of Jack onto the bed and then jumped off the bed onto the floor. Jack watched the door close and wondered what he should do.

Chapter 8

"Seth, be a dear and pour me another glass of wine, would you?" Carol asked her husband as she stood up from the stool she sat on. The party all sat or stood around the island in the middle of the kitchen, most of them turned or looked up at her. "I need to use the restroom."

"Sure thing dearie," Seth said and pushed himself away from the island, picked up her glass, and turned to look for the wine bottles.

Carol, as well as all the other party guests, were comfortable in Tom and Jill's house. She had no issues walking past the staircase and turning to go down the hall that led to the bathroom. The first-floor bathroom wasn't huge, but it was nice with a sink, toilet, and bathtub. Jill always decorated it according to the holiday or the season, and today was no different. Carol smiled at the Christmas shower curtain pulled closed and the red and green towels hanging on the towel rod as she lifted the toilet seat lid.

“Oh,” she said as her naked ass met the cold toilet seat. Carol sat there expelling her urine and looking around Jill’s bathroom. She opened the cabinet door under the sink and leaned forward to look at the contents inside. While she was nosing around she felt something tugging at her panties as they hung around her calves. Carol sat back up and looked down and screamed out when she saw an elf doll sitting in her panties, with a gleaming, metal fingernail file in its hands.

"Hi bitch, your pussy stinks," Butter-snap said, then jammed the metal file into her clit. Carol screamed again, much louder and higher this time. She jumped up off the toilet, flinging the elf out of her panties. The file stayed in place, buried in her clit.

Carol's first instinct was to pull the file out

of her, and she grabbed a hold of it and yanked. Blood sprayed from her wound and she screamed again as she made a move towards the door, pants, and underwear around her ankles. Butter-snap climbed up on the sink and when Carol saw him she freaked out, taking a step backward. Her garments around her ankles tripped her up and she lost her balance, falling backward as her arms windmilled.

Seeing her teetering there, unbalanced but not going anywhere just yet, Butter-snap leaped off of the sink and landed on Carol's chest. It was just the tipping point needed for her to go tumbling backward. She fell hard into the porcelain bathtub, her head bouncing off the tile wall as she impacted with the tub, something in her neck popped as her head bent cruelly forward.

Butter-snap rode Carol like she was a human surfboard as she crumpled into the bathtub. The elf turned to see the metal file still grasped in her hand, ripped the file from her clutches and turned back to look at her face. Carol's eyes were wide open but she was dazed.

"Say good night bitch!" Butter-snap said. He swung the file down from overhead and slammed the point into Carol's right eye. The eyeball exploded into a milky white goo that splattered the elf's clothing and ran down Carol's cheek.

Butter-snap placed one small foot in-between Carol's eyes, on the bridge of her nose, and the other foot on the other side of her right eye and yanked the fingernail file from the destroyed orb. She screamed again and tried to raise her hands to defend herself somehow, but nothing was working right, her limbs weren't obeying her. They lay there like dead fish, immobile and useless. He wasted no time in moving to the other eye. This one was closed as she screamed and wanted to flail about but couldn't. Butter-snap repeated the process, only this time the sharp, metal file pierced through the skin of her eyelid and then into her eyeball.

When the tiny elf pulled the file out this time, the thin flesh of her eyelid tore and Carol's eyeball came out intact, though still connected to

Carol via a bundle of wet, gooey nerves.

"Holy shit, will you look at that," Butter-snap said, looking at the eyeball. Realizing what he just said he started laughing. "My bad, guess you can't"

Butter-snap pushed the eyeball off of the fingernail file and let it fall, it caught on the nerves and dangled next to her face.

"Jesus Christ, I'm sick of the fucking screaming lady," the elf said. He raised the file again, and this time slammed it in her neck, right next to her esophagus, and yanked it back out. Blood spurted from the wound in a small arc and Carol's screams immediately turned into a garbled sound. Butter-snap stabbed her in the neck a couple more times, opening a decent-sized hole and finally she quit making any noise at all. Blood oozed from the enlarged wound in her throat, running down her body and into the tub, turning the bright porcelain from white to red.

"That's better," he said to her corpse. Butter-snap climbed up her leg and out of the bathtub.

Out in the kitchen, the party continued. The music had gotten louder when one of Seth's favorite songs came on and he just had to turn it up and sing along with it. Kelly was watching Seth as he swayed around the kitchen in a drunken dance when it occurred to her that Carol had been gone a while. She sat her wine glass on the counter where she was standing and backed out of the kitchen while watching Seth and smiling. Evan and Jill were clapping in rhythm with the music and Tom turned to see Kelly walk out of the room before turning back to the spectacle at hand.

Kelly turned the corner of the staircase and walked down the hall to the first-floor bathroom, and as she reached the door, her foot slipped on something. She had to throw her hand out to grab the door frame to keep from falling. She looked down and saw there were little spots of something wet on the floor. She wasn't sure what they were but decided to ignore them for now and deal with one thing at a time. She turned back to the bathroom door and knocked.

"Carol, everything okay in there?" she asked. She stood there a moment and listened, there was no answer so she knocked again. "Carol, Carol? Are you okay in there?"

Kelly tried the door knob and the door was unlocked.

"Carol, I'm coming in," Kelly said as she pushed the door open. Immediately she saw the blood on the floor in front of the toilet, and then her eyes went to the legs sticking out of the tub, pants, and panties wrapped around the ankles. She stepped into the room to get a better look at what had happened.

"Oh my god," she said, her hands clasped together at her chest. When she peered over the edge of the tub and saw Carol's ruined face, she flipped out. Kelly turned quickly and ran from the room. Her stomach immediately began to heave as she stumbled out into the hallway. Instinctively she put her hand up to try to catch the vomit as it spewed from her mouth, but her one hand couldn't hold it all and it spilled out onto the floor in front of her. Between the wetness already on the floor and her own sick, she slipped trying to hold herself up with the wall and fell onto her ass, hard.

Kelly rolled over onto her side, tears filling up her eyes as she reached behind her to rub her sore ass. She needed to get up and go tell the others about Carol, but when she put her hand on the floor to push herself up, she put her hand in her puke, and she started to dry heave, her stomach convulsing as she wretched. Kelly turned her head away from the puke as she continued to gag and through her tear-blurred vision she saw something down at the end of the hall. Its shape made it look like a small elf, maybe half a foot tall, just standing there staring at her. It had something in its hands, something shiny and sharp looking.

"What the heck is that?" she said aloud as she sat back up and wiped at her chin. Then, the little thing began walking toward her. Kelly's eyes went wide and she moved without even thinking, scooting backward on the floor. She smeared her sick under her as she moved and her hand slipped on the wet floor again, but she managed to pull herself into the bathroom and slammed the door behind her before whatever that was made it to her. She sat there with her back to the door and her eyes closed, not wanting to see Carol's dead body in the tub. Something sliced her wrist and she screamed out and moved away from the door, not wanting to get too close to the bathtub, but enough to turn around and look at what had cut her.

A flat metal object was sliding under the door, in a small arc back and forth. It looked like a fingernail file to Kelly, and it was obviously sharp. She held her wrist up to get a look at it, blood ran down from a nice cut across it.

“Fine you little bitch, hide in there with your friend, I'll get you later though,” a voice she didn’t recognize said from the other side of the door. Kelly started hyperventilating, she kept asking herself what was going on here.

Chapter 9

“I think I need another drink,” Seth said after the song on the radio switched.

"I'm not so sure of that,” Evan said to Tom, under his breath so no one else could hear. Tom just shook his head and took a drink from his screwdriver, which was now his fourth or fifth one. Seth moved over to the refrigerator to grab the orange juice out and Jill stood up from her seat at the island.

“Here let me do it, why don’t you take a load off after all that dancing around the kitchen,” she said to him with a smile, She took the OJ from his hand and he nodded to her.

“Okay, thanks,” he turned away from her

and then quickly turned back. “Make this one strong for me, Tom’s were kind of weak, I hardly feel buzzed right now.”

Jill smiled at him and nodded, but she didn’t have any plans to do that. Seth went back to where Tom and Evan were sitting at the island.

"I don’t know Seth, you kind of look like you're not feeling any pain right now,” Tom said with a laugh.

“What? No, I’m just getting started tonight!” he said enthusiastically and started moving his hips as he danced in place. Jill sat his screwdriver, which was mainly orange juice, down on the island in front of him. She walked around Seth, giving him a wide berth, and leaned in next to Tom.

“I’m going to go check on Jack, I'll be right back,” she said into his ear. He turned to her and kissed her cheek.

“Okay,” he said and watched her walk out of the kitchen.

“Your wife makes way better screwdrivers than you do pally,” Seth said. Tom turned to him and watched as he took a hardy drink from his glass. “I'm sorry, she's just a better bartender than you are. I guess OWW, my foot!” Seth screamed out and stepped away from the island.

Tom jumped up from his stool and ran around the island to see what was wrong with Seth.

“Seth, what's wrong?” Tom stopped when he saw Seth’s foot and the shiny metal thing sticking out from the top of it.

“What in the world?” Evan said as he stood next to Tom.

Trisha’s first instinct was to grab Carol and see what they could do to help Seth, but that's when she realized Carol wasn't there, and neither was Kelly. Where was everybody? She thought to herself.

“Oh god, it hurts, pull it out!” Seth screamed. He had his foot up now, in his hands, and he bounced around the kitchen on one foot. Tom and Evan looked at each other.

“Should we pull it out?” Evan asked.

“I don’t know, that seems like a bad idea,’

Tom said. “We need to get him still, calm him down. He's going to fall over and hurt himself worse.”

The two men moved to grab Seth, one on either side of him.

“How did this even happen? I mean, what is that even in his foot?” Evan asked, more out loud than to anyone in particular.

“I'm not sure,” Tom said. He grabbed Seth’s arm. “Seth, buddy, you need to calm down. Let us take a look at this.”

The two men grabbed Seth on either side and steadied him. They helped lower him to the ground, and the entire time he complained about how bad it hurt.

“I’ll get a cold rag, might help keep him from passing out,” Trisha said. She turned to the sink and began opening the drawers surrounding it. That’s when she saw the movement out of the corner of her eye. She looked at the counter and stopped. There was a small elf standing there, dressed in red but it was also covered in something that looked wet and sticky, and her first thought was cranberry sauce. Curious, she tilted her head, almost like a dog, and the little thing mimicked her. Behind her, she could hear the three men as they tried to figure things out. She turned from the elf to say something to them about this odd little creature and so didn't see Butter-snap pull a steak knife from the knife block directly next to him.

"Hey Tom," Trisha started, then she felt an incredible pain near her shoulder blade. She cried out and fell to her knees as she reached for whatever hit her back, not realizing there was a steak knife sticking out of her. Tom and Evan turned away from Seth to see what happened to Trisha. They watched her for a moment as she reached behind her with both arms, then Tom looked up and fell backward onto his ass.

"What in the hell? There's no way," he said. He couldn't believe it, Butter-snap was standing on his counter. His first thought was that Jack had been right.

"Tom, um, is that your Magic Elf?" Evan said, the words feeling stupid as they left his mouth. Tom nodded his head, unable to speak at that moment.

“Hello boys,” Butter-snap said to them. “The life of the party is here now, it’s time to really start having fun!”

“No, no, no, there's no way this is fucking happening,” Tom said, shaking his head slowly.

“What are you all doing, I still have this dang thing in my foot,” Seth said. He turned to see what Tom and Evan were looking at and his mouth dropped open. Butter-snap reached back and pulled another knife from the knife block and jumped down off the counter, landing on Trisha's back. Tom and Evan instinctively scooted back, even though they were a pretty good distance from Trisha. Butter-snap, his plastic face showing a sinister smile, plunged the steak knife into Trisha's throat from the back side, the sharp blade poked through and the tip stuck out the front of her neck. Seth felt his crotch warm as he let his bladder go.

"Trisha!" Evan yelled as he watched in horror what was happening to his wife.

Trisha fell forward as she grabbed at her throat. Butter-snap, still holding onto the knife handle, ripped the blade back out from Trisha's neck. Blood exploded from her throat onto the tiled kitchen floor, that finally got all the men moving.

Evan jumped up from the floor and stepped on Seth's hand. He was closest to the basement door and didn't hesitate to throw the door open and rush downstairs. Tom jumped up and grabbed a wine bottle off the island. He turned it upside down to use as a weapon and the remaining wine poured from the open mouth of the bottle. Seth stayed on the floor, but he scooted backward until his back hit a wall, leaving a trail of piss cooling on the floor in front of him.

Butter-snap stood there looking at the two men, deciding who he should attack first. He decided to just wing it and held the knife above his head as he ran toward them.

Tom jumped out of the little elf's way and took off toward the stairs, thinking only of his wife and son. Seth screamed out as the little thing ran toward him, the knife now repositioned so that he was holding the blade like he was jousting. Instead of doing something smart like trying to protect himself, Seth sat there screaming as Butter-snap ran into him, burying the knife in his ball sack and pinning his nuts to his taint, right in between his dick and his asshole. Seth began screaming and dropped his hands to his pierced privates just as Butter-snap pushed the knife down, the blade slicing through Seth and coming out in-between his ass cheeks, his asshole now much larger and his fleshy nut-sack split open in between his testicles. Blood filled the seat of his pants and he kicked his legs wildly like a toddler throwing a tantrum.

The little elf quickly moved away from Seth's flailing legs and positioned himself directly in front of the man.

“It's been a while since I’ve tried this trick, and obviously I was much bigger then,” Butter-snap said as he lifted the knife above his red Santa hat. He held it at the tip of the blade, his tiny hands pressing against either side of the blade.

With much of his strength, Butter-snap threw the knife at the screaming and crying Seth. It flew end over end until the blade slammed home, directly in the middle of Seth's forehead, smacking his head back against the cabinet. "Fuck yeah, still got it."

Butter-snap turned his attention to the basement door. He had his options now, he could go down there and take out the one guy, or he could go after Jack's parents. Also, there was the woman in the bathroom still. Part of him thought it might be fun to burn the house down with all of them in it, but he didn't think he could kill Jack for whatever reason. He didn't understand this stupid weird bond he had with the kid. It was almost like he really was part elf or something, and when the kid named him it attached them somehow. He sure as fuck didn't understand it like he didn't understand how he got there or anything. Once he was done killing this stupid family he was going to see about getting back to hell, getting back in his normal body, and getting back to fucking and killing the way he always had before, not as a little tiny, no cock having creature dressed in red.

“Ya know what, fuck it. I think I will try to burn this place to the ground,” Butter-snap said to himself as he made his way to the island in the middle of the kitchen. “And if any of these fuckers come out of hiding I'll just pick them off, easy as that.”

Easily climbing up one of the stools, Butter-snap reached the top of the island quickly. There, in the middle, in-between drink glasses and liquor bottles sat a candle Jill had lit earlier before everyone had arrived. Butter-snap kicked over wine glasses, the men’s tumblers they had been drinking out of, a bottle of vodka, and a bottle of red wine. The liquids mixed as they ran for the edges of the island and spilled over, dripping onto the floor. Lastly, Butter-snap kicked over the candle and watched as the flame immediately ignited the liquid and danced along the top of the island.

Butter-snap jumped across to the counter and made his way to the knife block as flames dripped from the island top to the tiled floor. He selected another knife from the knife block, this time choosing one a little bigger than a steak knife. Near the wooden knife block was a roll of paper towels, and seeing that gave Butter-snap an idea. He tossed the roll away from the flames but towards the basement door and leaped off the counter, landing on Trisha's back again. Her corpse let out a wheeze when he impacted and some blood spurted out from the hole in her neck. He noticed the flames were getting close to her and figured she'd be going up soon.

The little elf pushed a stool across the floor to the basement door and stopped with it at the edge of the door. Butter-snap climbed up the stool and turned the doorknob and pulled the door open. He climbed back down, grabbed the roll of paper towels, and touched one end of it to the fire. Back at the basement door, he stood at the edge of the stairs and pushed the paper towels down into the depths. The flaming roll un-spooled as it bounced down each stair. Butter-snap slammed the door closed and climbed back up the stool where he turned the latch in the door knob to lock the door.

Down in the darkness of the basement, Evan cowered behind the washer and dryer in the laundry, which was located in the farthest corner of the basement. He heard the sound of the door opening and covered his head with his arms like he thought something was attacking him and pissed himself. He stayed in that position while he heard the sound of something softly falling down the basement stairs and still huddled like that as he heard the basement door close and then a click.

He had no idea what was happening out there in the rest of the basement, nor what was happening upstairs, he cowered in his cooling piss, his mind conjuring up images of demonic killer elves with razor-sharp teeth hunting for him in the darkness.

Chapter 10

"Jill!" Tom yelled once he was upstairs and turning the corner to head to Jack's room "Jill!"

Jill came out of Jack's room and meet Tom in the hallway. She looked at his frantic face and the wine bottle in his hand.

"Tom, what is it? Jack's sleeping, you're going to wake him up," she said with some irritation. Tom took a second to catch his breath and looked back over his shoulder like he expected someone to have followed him up the stairs.

"Jack was telling the truth about the elf," Tom said when he turned back to her.

"What, what the hell does that mean?"

"Remember when he said the elf was in his room after we got him, I think he was telling the truth."

"The toy elf, Butter-snap?" Jill asked, trying to figure out what Tom was raving about. She thought he was beginning to sound like a loon.

"Mother fucker, I hate that name!" A voice from behind Tom said. They both looked towards the stairs and there, in all of his four or so inches tall glory, covered in blood, was Butter-snap. "You're stupid fucking kid could have named me anything, and he chose the dumbest fucking name possible."

"What the hell is this?" Jill asked like she just didn't get what was happening.

"Hey bitch, we haven't been properly introduced. I'm your stupid fucking scout elf from hell. I'm here to rape and kill you," Butter-snap flipped the knife in his hand menacingly. "And not necessarily in that order."

"Jill, get back into Jack's room and lock

the door," Tom said, pushing his wife back away from them.

"Tom," Jill started.

"Just do it!" Tom shouted. "This thing is small, but I watched it murder Trisha, you don't know what it's capable of."

Reluctantly, Jill did what her husband told her to do.

Tom didn't take his eyes off of the elf but heard the door shut and the lock click behind him. He adjusted his grip on the neck of the bottle as the two squared off.

"Well, come on Tom, make your move pussy," Butter-snap sneered at him. Tom took the bait, in his head he couldn't get past the fact that it was just a little toy elf. He could just step on it, or grab it and rip it in half, right? He lunged at the elf, swinging the wine bottle down as he went. Butter-snap was fast, faster than Tom anticipated anyway, and he easily dodged the bottle, which shattered on impact on the hardwood floor. Butter-snap ran in between Tom's legs and sliced the inside of his left ankle with the knife. Tom screamed out, his momentum causing him to fall forward and he couldn't find anything to grab to stop him from falling as he hit the first step of the staircase and began tumbling down.

Everything was rolling past in his vision, first the stairs, then the second-floor landing, then the ceiling above the stairs with the light that hung down from a chain, and then the bottom of the stairs, over and over as he tumbled down, literally head over heels. When Tom finally stopped, he hit the floor hard, his head bouncing off the hardwood once before settling back down with a thud. Tom lost consciousness from the impact and lay there, splayed out, his legs still on the bottom stairs.

Butter-snap watched Tom as he rolled down the stairs, it was a development he hadn't anticipated, but he loved it.

He hoped that Tom broke his neck in the fall and maybe lay paralyzed on the floor now, or at least broke some bones on the way down. He was a little disappointed that none of his bones snapped and broke through his skin though.

'Can't have it all,' he thought.

He turned away from Tom and the staircase and started walking toward Jack's room, dragging the knife on the floor as he walked.

Chapter 11

Jill sat on Jack's bed cradling the boy. She rocked back and forth, holding on to him and patting the back of his head. The small, twin-sized bed creaked with her movements, other than that the room was silent. She could hear some of the tussle outside in the hallway, and she hoped Tom got the better of the little thing with the knife, but she had no way of knowing, She just had to sit and wait for it to be over. Something slammed into the bedroom door and she jumped and screamed out.

"Tom?" she asked, hesitantly. She waited in silence for a moment before asking again. "Tom, is that you?"

She was answered by another slam against the door, then another, and then another. On the fifth hit, a knife blade broke through towards the bottom of the door, a few inches from the ground. Jill screamed out and jumped off of the bed, pulling Jack with her. The blade disappeared, then broke back through, more of it showing through the wood of the door this time. Jill screamed again, louder and higher with each hit against the door, and squeezed Jack tighter and tighter against her chest. The blade just kept disappearing and reappearing with each hit, until a healthy chunk of wood broke out of the door and Butter-snap crawled through the ragged hole. Jill looked around desperately for a weapon of some kind.

“Alright, now it's playtime,” Butter-snap sneered. He slowly made his way across the room, dragging the large knife on the ground behind him.

Jill didn’t want to let go of Jack, but there was a toy fire truck to the right of her. Jill let go of the boy reluctantly and reached down for the long, bright red truck. She looped her fingers into the front of the toy, where the windshield would normally be on a regular, full-sized fire truck. This toy, on the other hand, was designed to be able to place action figures in the cab so that you could pretend they were driving. Jill picked the toy truck up by the cab and the rear portion, with the ladder that actually extended, swung down where it was hinged to the cab. Jill attempted to throw the fire truck but the swinging ladder end threw off her balance and when she let go of the toy truck, it weakly fell next to the deranged-looking, killer elf.

"What the fuck was that lady? If that's all you've got, you might as well just lay down on the floor and let me have you," Butter-snap said as he continued walking toward her. "I promise you, it will feel really good when I get all up inside your pussy."

Jill pulled Jack toward her again, her hands going to his ears as she tried to protect him from the filthy things the elf was saying.

Thinking only of protecting her son, Jill kicked out at the little elf as he approached.

Having planned on spending a comfortable evening with friends at her own house, Jill was always more comfortable without shoes or socks on. So, as she kicked out towards Butter-snap he swung the razor-sharp kitchen knife slicing the bottom pad of her bare foot. Blood immediately squirted from the wound as Jill screamed out in pain. Jack also cried out, from both fear of the situation and his mother's pain. Jill pulled her foot back away from the elf and somehow managed to stay upright, partially leaning on her son. But, she was at a loss for what to do to protect them from the tiny killer. Jack ended up being the one thinking quickly on his feet as he grabbed his comforter off the bed and tossed it over the elf.

"Hey, what the fuck is this shit?" they heard the little voice say from underneath the comforter. Jill didn't waste any time and kicked out at the little thing a second time. This time, the little elf rolled across the room, covered by the comforter and Jill grabbed Jack into her arms and limped as fast as she could from the room.

Chapter 12

Tom slowly opened his eyes and the first thing he noticed was the smell. Something was burning and he was confused. At first, he thought it may be the weekend and Jill had let him sleep in while she decided to make breakfast for the family. Clearly, something she was cooking was not going to be edible now, Tom thought as he lay there on the hardwood floor. He didn't usually like to sleep on his stomach and thought it was weird to wake like this, drool was running down the side of his face and when he lifted his head he could feel the drool stringing down to the floor. That's when it started to hit him, the hardwood floor was under him, so he wasn't in bed. It wasn't Saturday, he wasn't getting ready to get a home-cooked breakfast. No, he just woke up from being knocked unconscious from falling down the stairs, which was caused by a psychotic killer elf toy. Things could not be any weirder than that, period.

Tom pushed his upper body up from the floor, and he noticed his legs were still laying on the bottom steps of the staircase. He felt sore pretty much all over his body but he was surprised that nothing felt broken. For the moment, Tom felt like he got very, very lucky.

Once he was fully erect he had to lean against the wall to catch his bearings. His head swam and his vision was a little fucked up, and he was dizzy. The smell of burning and smoke was strong once he stood up and he was immediately concerned about what was on fire, his first thought was the house.

Tom pushed himself off the wall and walked around the staircase. In front of him, the kitchen was ablaze.

"Holy shit," he said and then he spun

around when he heard a noise from behind him, expecting the elf to be coming to finish him off.

Kelly walked around the corner and saw Tom and screamed out with surprise.

"Oh my god, Tom!" Kelly yelled.

"Kelly! What's going on? Where did you come from?"

"I was in the bathroom, Karen is in there. She's dead. I was trapped in there because, this is going to sound crazy, you're not gonna believe me…"

"There's a killer toy elf on the loose," Tom said to her, deadpan.

"Oh, so you know. Okay then, I guess I'm not crazy, thank God for that," Kelly said. "But it tried to kill me. It had me trapped in the bathroom and I've been in there all this time but I started smelling the smoke and thought maybe the house was on fire, so I came out and that's when I ran into you."

"That little bastard is upstairs with Jill and Jack, I have to go get them," Tom said to her. "You need to get out of here while you still can, call the fire department, the police, whatever."

Tom turned from her and started for the stairs when he looked up to see Jill coming down the stairs carrying Jack.

"Oh my God, you guys are okay?" Asked Tom, as he held out his arms and grabbed his wife and son once they reached the bottom of the steps.

"Yes, we're okay, but he's probably right behind us!" Jill said to him in a panic.

Tom took the boy from her arms and noticed Kelly was still standing there.

"We need to get out of here, now," Tom said to the group.

With his free hand, Tom grabbed Jill's hand and began to pull her away from the staircase so they could run through the living room and out the front door. But, just then they heard a scream and turned to see the little red elf flying down from the second floor with the knife in his small hands. The knife, still in Butter-snap's hands, impaled into the top of Kelly's skull with a loud thunk.

She didn't make a sound, didn't scream at

all. Her eyes just rolled up into her head like she was looking up to see what hit her. Then Kelly collapsed to the floor dead.

"Oh, no, you motherfuckers. You're not getting away that easy," Butter-snap said as he attempted to wrench the blade from Kelly's skull.

Seeing the little elf defenseless, Tom dropped Jack to his feet on the floor next to him and reached down to grab the demonic doll. Just as he was inches away from grabbing him, Butter-snap managed to rip the knife free and swung it up in an arc and Tom lost three-quarters of his index finger, half of his middle finger, and the tip of his ring finger on his right hand. The severed digits went flying through the air as Tom, Jill, and Jack all screamed out. Tom's finger stumps sprayed blood like little tiny fire hoses as Tom pulled his wounded hand to his chest and fell backward on his ass from the surprise of the attack.

"Oh yeah bitch, you're not getting me that easy!" Butter-snap yelled as he lunged from Kelly's head out toward Tom. Tom tried to move out of the little elf's path, but between the shock of the attack and the blood loss, he was too slow. As Butter-snap flew through the air holding his kitchen knife up like some crazed action movie star, the sharp steel pierced into the meat next to Tom's shoulder, right in between his shoulder joint and his pectoral muscle. Tom screamed out again, but this time he was able to reach up and back hand the elf off of him, the knife stayed buried in place.

"Tom!" Jill screamed as she watched her husband get stabbed after he just lost some of his fingers. She grabbed Tom under his armpit on the good shoulder and helped him stand up. Tom looked down at the knife handle sticking out from his body.

"Pull it out!" he screamed at her. She shook her head no.

"You might bleed out, and we need to run!" Jill yelled back at him. She looked around frantically to see where the little elf went when Tom knocked him away, but she didn't see him. There was blood everywhere, from her foot,

Kelly's head, and Tom's fingers, and there were little feet prints through it leading around the staircase. “Come on, let's go now!”

She grabbed Tom around the waist to help him and waved for Jack to follow. Their son just stood there in place, eyes bulged out huge. Jill opened her mouth to say something to him, to tell him to come on, let’s go, when Butter-snap appeared crawling up his back and resting on the boy's shoulder. He had a pair of small scissors she instantly recognized as the ones she used to trim Jack's hair, which she usually kept in the bathroom. Butter-snap put the points against Jack’s jugular.

“One more step and the boy gets it,” he said to Tom and Jill. They stood there, frozen in fear. The heat from the fire in the kitchen was reaching out to where they stood. Jill looked over her shoulder towards it feeling like the flames were getting closer to them. Something loud hit somewhere in the kitchen and they all jumped. The scissor tips nicked Jack’s neck and Butter-snap recoiled. The loud bang from the kitchen came again, and again.

Jack was terrified of the little elf on his shoulder, and whatever the sharp thing was that was poking him in the neck that he couldn't see. But he felt Butter-snap recoil when he stabbed him, and he remembered what the elf had said before, about being bonded together and he thought he knew what that meant. The elf couldn't hurt him.

Deciding to take his chance in the hopes of saving his mom and dad, Jack reached up and grabbed Butter-snap. He felt gross and sticky since he was covered in blood. The shock of being grabbed caused him to drop the scissors.

"Get off of me you little motherfucker!" Butter-snap screamed.

Without putting much thought into what exactly he was doing, Jack tossed the little elf like he was discarding a rag doll, towards the inferno that was the kitchen. Jill and Tom turned to follow Butter-snaps trajectory as he flew through the air, all the way until he landed at the edge of the kitchen. He was close enough to the fire that it was singeing the cloth outfit he wore, but not close enough that he was truly harmed.

"Oh you are going to get it you little pussy bitch," Butter-snap yelled toward the boy. But he knew that was a lie, he couldn't hurt the boy, stupid weird fucking bond and all, so he turned his attention toward Jack's parents.

Tom and Jill took a step back as if they were synchronized, but before the tiny elf could make a move, there was another loud bang from deep in the kitchen, and an ember bounced out and landed on Buttersnap's back. Immediately a flame broke out up his back, igniting his little red hat too. The elf screamed out and rolled on the ground, stuffing the fire out rather quickly, to Tom and his family's disappointment.

Butter-snap stood back up and dusted himself off, his little cap falling off into black ashes.

"Ha, thought I was done for didn't you fuckers?" The demonic elf said, stepping toward them. Tom pushed his wife back, and she in turn blocked their son. Tom didn't know what else to do, so he grabbed the handle of the knife sticking out of him and tried to pull the blade free. He screamed out and his legs went wobbly, Jill grabbed him to help him stay on his feet. That wasn't going to work.

The loud banging from the kitchen became more frantic and Jill thought it sounded like someone pounding on a door. Butter-snap inched his way towards the frightened family just as on the other side of the kitchen the basement door flew open and a person completely covered in flames came barreling through. Everyone looked up from the elf to see Evan, flames dancing from everywhere on his body, as he ran toward them, screaming like a maniac. Butter-snap leaped off the floor, aiming toward Tom as Evan ran out of the kitchen, grabbed the elf in mid-air, and threw him into the burning inferno. Then, the man on fire collapsed to the floor. Flames spread from his charred flesh and ran across the hardwood of the hallway, licking up the walls.

"Look," Jack said, pointing into the kitchen. Tom and Jill followed where his finger was pointing and saw Butter-snap stand up near the island in the middle of the kitchen. His little body was completely engulfed in flames much like Evan was. The tiny elf took one, two steps toward them. He fell to his knees before standing up again.

"How in the hell is he still going?" Jill asked.

They watched as the elf took two more steps before falling face down on the tiled floor.

"I think that's it now," Tom said. "Let's get out of here before we burn to death too."

Jill supported Tom's weight on his side without the knife protruding from his body, and they slowly made their way to the front door, all the while the flames danced at their backs, threatening to overtake them if they didn't get out fast enough.

Once outside in the freezing winter night, they could hear the sirens of firetrucks screaming as they neared their house. The three of them turned and watched their home as it succumbed to the flames rising out of the roof and blasting out windows. It was the only home they knew, but even still, they hugged each other tight, comforted by the fact that at least they made it out alive. Cars pulled up in the street in front of the house behind them and they could hear the shouts and yelling behind them, but they weren't ready to turn away from what remained of their home yet.

Another window burst outward, this one in the front of the house, and a screaming, smoldering object flew through the air toward them. The little ball of fire slammed into Tom before anyone could realize it was a charred black, but still alive, Butter-snap. The elf grabbed the knife that was still protruding from Tom's pectoral muscle and yanked it out with surprising strength, flinging a gusher of blood into the air. Jill and Jack were screaming as the little demon began to repeatedly drive the knife into Tom's chest and pull it back out, slamming it over and over into his flesh. Blood was everywhere, coating Jill and Jack both as the burnt-to-a-crisp elf maniacally hacked away at Tom as he fell backward onto the cold ground.

Gunshots rang out through the night as the blackened little doll flew backward off of Tom's chest, doing somersaults through the air and landing in the grass just a foot away from Tom's lifeless body.

"What the fuck was that?" A young police officer said, as he stood in a shooter's stance, his service pistol still pointing outward, smoke rising from the barrel.

Jill and Jack fell to the ground on their knees, both grabbing and hugging Tom's now cooling corpse.

ABOUT THE AUTHOR

Matthew Vaughn is the author of The ADHD Vampire, Mother Fucking Black Skull of Death, Hellsworld Hotel, and 30 Minutes or Less. With his brother, Edward Vaughn, they edited and compiled The Classics Never Die! An Anthology of Old School Movie Monsters for their own press, Red All Over Books.

He lives in Shelbyville, Kentucky and is the father of five kids, yet he and his wife are just big kids too. By day he maintains machines and robots, by night he is a writer of Bizarro and Horror fiction. You can keep up with his work at:

http://authormatthewvaughn.com/

https://www.facebook.com/

AuthorMatthewVaughn

https://twitter.com/mcvaughn138

https://www.instagram.com/m_f_n_black_skull_of_death

RED ALL OVER BOOKS

Printed in Great Britain
by Amazon

51184268R00069